Chri

Jugg ...my

CA 1405 20485(

KT-174-539

Dun Laoghaire-Rathdown Libraries
CABINTEELY LIBRARY
Inv/04 : I71J   Price £5.97
Title: Juggling with Jeremy
Class: JF

Cabin...
Te. 2

Items to b
The loan
is a wait.n
Fines, as
overdue .om
Damage to, or

05. JAN
13. JA

17. FEB

04 MAR 05

04 AP

05 MAY

BAINTE DEN STOC

WITHDRAWN FROM
DÚN LAOGHAIRE-RATHDOWN COUNTY
LIBRARY STOCK

First published in Great Britain 1996
This edition published in 2002
by Egmont Books Limited
239 Kensington High St, London W8 6SA
Published in hardback by Heinemann Library,
a division of Reed Educational and Professional Publishing Ltd
by arrangement with Egmont Books Limited
Text copyright © Chris d'Lacey 1996
Illustrations copyright © Gus Clarke 1996
The author and illustrator have asserted their moral rights
Paperback ISBN 1 4052 0485 0
Hardback ISBN 0 434 97460 9
10 9 8 7 6 5 4 3 2 1
A CIP catalogue record for this title
is available from the British Library.
Printed and bound in the U.A.E.
This book is sold subject to the condition
that it shall not, by way of trade or otherwise,
be lent, resold, hired out, or otherwise circulated
without the publisher's prior consent in any form
of binding or cover other than that in which
it is published and without a similar condition
including this condition being imposed on
the subsequent purchaser.

Chris d'Lacey • Gus Clarke

Juggling with Jeremy

BLue Bananas

For Marshall

Who is also quite a good weight

C. d'L.

One day Jeremy was watching T.V.

'Mu-um! I want to be a juggler!' he cried.

Mum was taking clothes
from the tumble dryer.
Some clothes were stacked on
the ironing board. She was busy.
She wasn't really listening to Jeremy.

Jeremy picked up three bundles of socks.

They were quite a good weight.

He started to throw the

socks into the air.

The socks went everywhere.

One lot dropped into the washing up –

Another lot dropped

into the dog's bowl –

Jeremy managed to catch

the other bundle.

Mum frowned darkly.

Jeremy blushed.

'Come on,' said Mum, 'we're going

shopping.'

Jeremy liked the supermarket.

He liked to push the

shopping trolley.

He liked
to bump
other people's
trolleys.

11

But today he just wanted to juggle.

Mum bought fish and biscuits and beans. Then she stopped by the egg counter. She opened a box of eggs. She looked at the eggs to check they weren't cracked.

Jeremy took three eggs. They were quite a good weight. Jeremy tossed the eggs into the air.

One came down on the supermarket floor –

splat! Another came down

on the head of the supermarket

manager – *double splat!*

Jeremy managed to catch the other egg.

The supermarket manager was very angry. An egg yolk was running down his nose. It looked as if he'd got a horrible cold.

No throwing eggs at the Manager, please!

I'm VERY angry!

Mum made Jeremy hold onto the trolley after that.

On the way home, Mum stopped at
the garage to buy some petrol.
Jeremy liked the garage.
He liked to watch the petrol pumps
working. He liked to see dirty cars
going into the carwash and clean
cars coming out.

But today he just wanted to juggle.

Mum went into the garage to pay for the petrol. Jeremy went with her. There was another mum there, with her little girl. The little girl was holding some cuddly toys. She had a bear, a rabbit and a chimpanzee.

Say hello to Bingo.

Jeremy frowned. He didn't think much of cuddly toys. But he took them anyway. He took them outside. The toys were a good weight. Not bad for . . .

. . . juggling.

Jeremy threw the toys into the air. The little girl laughed.

The chimp landed on the petrol station roof – *douf!*

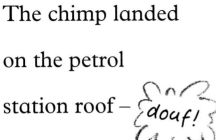

The rabbit dropped into a passing truck – *double douf!*

Jeremy managed to catch the bear.

The little girl cried. Her mum was
very angry. She didn't smile at
Jeremy's mum any more. Jeremy's
mum blushed. She bought the little girl a
nice new rabbit from the garage display.

The petrol attendant got Bingo off the roof. Jeremy had to sit in the car after that.

Mum was cross. 'You need a
day in the country,' she said.

'What's in the country?' Jeremy asked.

'Flowers and cows,' Mum replied.

Jeremy was bored. There were LOTS of flowers and cows in the country.

Trees, too…

And hedges.

And fields.

There was nothing to juggle with.

Then Mum said, 'Shall we visit the

farm park?'

The farm park was brilliant.

Jeremy fed the goats and sheep from

his hands.

He watched the cows being milked.

He sat in a tractor and
steered the wheel.

But what he really
wanted to do was juggle.

Then he saw a sign that said:

Working
Blacksmith

The blacksmith was putting horseshoes
on a horse. The blacksmith's name was
Tiny Tom. But he wasn't tiny.
His muscles were huge.

Tiny Tom smiled at Jeremy.

'Would you like to pass me some

horseshoes?' he said.

Jeremy picked up three horseshoes
from the pile. He held them in his
hands. They were a *very* good weight.
Just right for . . .

35

. . . juggling. Jeremy tossed the horseshoes in the air. One landed on the blacksmith's anvil – *crash!* Another went through the window of his workshop – *double crash!*

Jeremy managed to catch the other shoe.

Tiny Tom was very angry.

Jeremy's mum blushed. 'I'm sorry,'
she said. 'He's been doing that all day.

I wish he'd stop it.'

She told Tom about the socks and the eggs
and the toys.

'I can make him stop it,' said Tom.

Tom went across the yard.

He picked up two big sacks of

grain. He carried the grain into a

field. 'Would you like to see me juggle

these sacks?' he said.

'Yes, PLEASE!' said Jeremy.

'But you've only got two.'

'So I have,' Tom grinned. 'Now what

weighs the same as a sack of grain?'

A hundred tins of dog food?

A thousand bits of cheese?

A million mice?!

It wasn't any of these things.

It was Jeremy!

Before anyone could speak, Jeremy and the sacks were flying through the air. Tiny Tom was a very good juggler.

Almost...

A sack came down with a thud on the grass.

Jeremy sailed through the air
and landed safely
in a haystack.

Tiny Tom managed to catch the other sack.

After all that, Jeremy didn't want to juggle any more. He wanted a safer hobby. 'How about knitting?' Mum suggested. Jeremy thought that sounded boring . . .

Until he saw the balls of wool in Mum's

basket!

Leabharlanna Dhúin Laoghaire · Ráth An Dúin